The Pesky Bunnies of BeWILDerwood

TOM BLOFELD

Illustrated by
STEVE PEARCE

HOLLY DAY & BUMP PUBLISHING

First published in 2014 by
Holly Day & Bump Publishing
BeWILDerwood, Horning Road, Hoveton
Norwich NR12 8JW
BeWILDerwood.co.uk

First Edition
Copyright © Tom Blofeld 2014

ISBN: 978-0-9555543-4-6

Designed & Typeset in Great Britain by Aaron Fickling
Printed in Great Britain by Barnwell Print Ltd.

Other BeWILDerbooks

Swampy opened one eye very carefully. Then he yawned and stretched his arms as wide as they would go. All of his blankets fell off the bed as he stretched, and when he tried to pull them back up, he fell out of bed with a clump.

"Time to get up, I suppose," he decided.

So he did.

It was very early morning in Bewilderwood. Spring was just nudging winter away with its little green shoots and fluffy white blossoms. There was a soft mist hanging over the marshes where Swampy lived, and the white shrouded sun was low in the sky.

Feeling a little chilly, Swampy felt that breakfast would be exactly the thing to warm him up. But when he looked in the cupboard there was nothing there, not even a dried sliverfish. He would have to go and catch his own breakfast today.

He unhooked his fishing pole from its place above his door and, after putting on an extra thick waistcoat, he shuffled out of his house and made his way to the main platform in the Boggle village. This was the place where the Boggles had most of their feasts and Swampy could almost smell the aroma of sweetsludge pie and mudwort jelly. But there was no feast today and the tables were empty.

He made his way down towards his boat and for just a second a tiny robin danced around his head and then vanished back into the mist. Swampy thought it might be Rosie, the Witch's special pet bird, but he didn't see the Witch anywhere.

He clumped off into the marshes, clambered into his boat and poled sleepily towards the pongy ponds. They were the best fishing grounds. But in the thick fog he must have lost his way a little because he bumped into a large sedge tussock by mistake.

As he was untangling the prow of his little boat, his eye was caught by something very tall and thin swaying in the distant mist-shrouded woods. He peered at the snake-like animal, if that's what it was, but he couldn't make it out properly. It didn't look like anything he had ever seen in Bewilderwood before, and it did seem to be an animal because he could dimly hear it making hundreds of little squeaky noises.

He tied his boat up quietly and tip-toed nervously through the marshes and into the wood to get a closer look.

What he saw astonished him.

The snake wasn't a snake at all. Instead, it was lots and lots of bunnies. Only they weren't doing what bunnies usually do. They were standing on top of each other's heads forming a long ladder of rabbits reaching high up into the branches of the trees. The very top rabbit seemed to be scooping some colourful things out of the twigs and putting them into a string bag.

"Hello there!" called Swampy, waving at the swaying pile of bunnies.

His voice was like a sudden shock in the cloudy stillness, and the effect was electric. Suddenly, the ladder collapsed and the marsh was alive with scampering white tails and flashing paws. Rabbits were bouncing everywhere, some crashing into each other and rolling head over heels before they hopped and scattered into the vegetation.

In seconds, there was no one there, except for Swampy who just stood and scratched his tummy as he wondered what to make of it all.

He decided he ought to go and have a chat with the nice Bewilderwood Witch to see if she knew why the bunnies were acting so oddly. But first he would catch his breakfast, as it was never a good idea to do anything on an empty stomach.

On the main Boggle platform, a crowd was forming, and Swampy had to push his way through it to see what was going on. In the middle of the crowd was the Witch, and she was looking very stern.

"I've got an announcement," she was saying. "And I'm quite cross about it. Somebody has been stealing all of my eggs. I'd like them to stop doing it."

Everybody gasped. It was rather a brave thing to steal something from the Witch and Boggles weren't very brave. Who could have been so audacious?

"I've been helping hide colourful eggs for the great Easter egg hunt," the Witch went on. "But no sooner do I hide the eggs than somebody takes them."

There was a commotion. Small Boggles blamed other small Boggles. A very old Boggle called Ticklechin began to try to tell everyone about a time when he was a boy and had once lost a sock. Nobody listened to him though. It took some time before the Witch managed to quiet everyone down.

"I know it can't be anyone here because the egg stealing mostly happens when you are all tucked up in your beds," she explained.

"But keep your eyes peeled for anything odd."

Swampy felt that with all of this trouble going on, perhaps the Witch might not want to be bothered with questions about rabbits forming bunny ladders. Instead, he and many of the other Boggles headed out into the marshes and waterways to see if they could find any clues to explain this great mystery.

A long way away from the Boggle village, deep in the Scary Lake, Mildred the crocklebog was blowing bubbles underwater. Circling her under the murky surface was a much smaller crocklebog. Only the tip of her tail was visible above the surface. She was called Minty and the two crocklebogs were making up a synchronized swimming routine together. This was the grand finale in which Minty's tail drew an egg and Mildred's bubbles coloured it in.

But they kept bumping into each other so it wasn't quite right yet.

"We're hopeleth," complained Mildred. She had a lisp which made her sound friendly.

"It is jolly difficult," agreed her small niece, Minty. "Maybe we should just wave flowers about instead, like we usually do?"

"But it'th an egg party," protested Mildred. "And if we do have flowerth then you generally eat them all before the show."

"I don't always. Well not the stalks, anyway. But the petals do taste so delicious and it's hard not to have a little nibble. Especially those scrummy yellow swamp ones," explained Minty. "Ooh look, there's Swampy coming over in his boat. Let's ask him what water-dance he thinks we should do."

The two crocklebogs waved and began to swim over to the little Boggle in his craft. He was trying to pole it back towards the bushes as fast as he could because Mildred often sank boats due to her habit of splooshing great jets of water out of her nose when she got excited. But the crocklebogs were quicker than he was, and they met him in the open water. Just as Swampy feared, Mildred did her great wet sploosh but luckily most of the water missed Swampy or his boat. Soon, the three of them were chatting away like the great friends they really were.

Swampy let them both know about all the exciting things that had happened that morning at the village. Minty made squeaky "ooh! and aah!" noises when she heard that the Witch was cross. But when Swampy came to the part about stealing the brightly coloured eggs, she went rather quiet. When the story had finished, Minty coughed and then, sounding very guilty, she announced that she might know a tiny something about those eggs.

"I was only trying to help though," Minty insisted. "Those poor bunnies seemed to have so many and I thought they might need help carrying them."

"You mean the rabbits took all the eggs?" said Swampy. "That must have been what I saw them doing this morning. I thought they were taking something. But why would bunnies steal eggs? They don't even like eggs."

"Well, they might like these ones. They taste yummy. They're made of chocolate, you see. I tried one or two," said Minty, licking some of her many teeth.

"Do you know where they might have taken them?" asked Mildred. "We ought to go and tell them they are naughty and mutht give them all back."

"Well I know where they are. But I don't know if they'll give them back. They don't talk like we do, so they might not understand us either. And they do bounce an awful lot. They are really quite frisky," replied Minty.

After a quick chat, the three friends agreed that the best thing they could do was to find the rabbits anyway and at least try to get them to give back the eggs. So Mildred took the bow rope of Swampy's boat in her teeth and pulled it along as she followed Minty to the place where the eggs were hidden.

They headed to the farthest shore where the bare alder trees were covered with grey lichen. At this time of year there weren't leaves to hide the swimming birds and a couple of coots bustled out of the low-hanging twigs and scuttled loudly across the water.

They tied up Swampy's boat and made their way into the wild marsh. Swampy had to jump along the islands made by the alder trunks, but he was a Marsh Boggle and found that quite easy.

Then they clambered along a narrow trail on the edge of the marsh. It had a sign saying it was called The Pointless Path. At the end, the path led up to the grassy picnic grounds. Here, a few daffodils were nodding their bright yellow heads in the milky sun, and Minty ate one or two of them as she passed.

The picnic grounds were deserted. Around the edge of the open grass some May trees were showing off their delicate white blossoms.

Behind them were piles of thick spiky brambles, and Minty searched for a hole at the bottom of one of these bushes. The soil beneath the hole had been dug away by the rabbits so all three of them could wriggle through it comfortably. They found they were in a clearing surrounded on all sides by tall tangled bramble bushes. The floor of the open space was covered in soft, spongy, grey-green moss. This moss was covered in sleeping furry bunny rabbits.

In the very centre of the clearing, there stood a huge pile of brightly coloured eggs. Right at the top of the pile was draped a large bunny. It was sleeping on its back with its large furry white tummy moving up and down slowly in time to the sound of gentle snores.

"Ahem," said Mildred, clearing her throat. She was about to say more but for the second time that day a slight noise had a huge effect.

The startled bunnies awoke to find two green crocklebogs in their lair. One of them was huge. They panicked. The light mossy clearing became a blurred mass of bouncing ears and tails as an explosion of rabbits shot in every direction, including up. Each bunny seemed to be bouncing at a different angle and speed, but as they pinged about they all managed to grab an egg and then they disappeared with it in a flurry of legs and tails, deep into the thorny brambles and beyond.

Swampy and the Crocklebogs were suddenly alone except for the rabbit who had been snoring on top of the pile of eggs. He was still sleeping. All the bright eggs were gone except the one the rabbit was laying on, which was now alone on the bare moss. The bunny snored happily, murmured something in his sleep and then rolled over, cuddling the last egg as he turned.

"I'll just wake this pesky bunny up, shall I?" asked Minty, poking him in the tummy with a gentle claw. But the bunny kept on snoring contentedly. He clung onto the egg tightly in his sleep, so Minty couldn't pull it away. She gave up trying.

"Now we've lost those eggs again," pointed out a sad Swampy. "I was rather hoping to try one or two."

"I think we'd better go and tell the Witch about what we've dithcovered," suggested Mildred. "I wonder where she might be."

Then Swampy remembered he had a special pipe the Witch had given him during one of his earlier adventures. There was a strange tune she had taught him. If he played it, and if the Witch was available, she would come and find him. He blew a rather spooky melody through the pipe.

This turned out to be the thing that woke up the final rabbit. It opened an eye lazily, then, tucking its egg under its front leg, it hopped slowly away into the bushes. Not even Minty tried to stop it. They were alone now and stood in silence.

"Maybe the Witch can't hear us in these thick bushes," worried Swampy.

Suddenly, a gentle voice behind him asked; "Did anybody need me?"

The Witch had arrived. Minty was delighted to see her and her fluttering robin.

"We've found the eggs you wanted, only we lost them and the bunnies have them and they are delicious and we didn't get to eat any. None at all." Minty explained.

"Yes, I can see that," smiled the Witch.

Swampy and Mildred told her about the bunnies a bit more clearly. The Witch nodded.

"Well, at least we have solved our mystery. Unfortunately I don't know how to talk to bunnies or how to get them to give the eggs back. They speak a very strange language and I could never learn it.

The Witch turned to Swampy. "Would you go back to the Boggle village and ask your friends to build a house for a special friend of mine to stay in? And tell everyone to prepare for a big party too. One with lots of chocolate eggs to eat."

Swampy nodded and smiled, and then, somehow, the Witch was gone. She didn't exactly disappear but just sort of shimmered away when they weren't looking at her. Mildred, Minty and Swampy were alone again in the empty clearing.

They wriggled back out to the picnic grounds, and then rushed back to the Boggle village with their news.

The next day the Boggles got to work. They decided to make an egg-shaped house for the Witch's friend, as it was to be an egg party. They put it near the village by the dancing green. Then the Twiggles helped decorate it with a huge bow. It was all done by lunch.

Then everybody prepared for the feast. Swampy's mum made sweetsludge pies as it isn't really a party without a bit of sweetsludge pie. The smaller Boggles and Twiggles hung out bunting. Old Ticklechin sat in his great chair and polished his ear trumpet while he watched all the activity.

Soon the Witch arrived. She was holding the paw of the largest, whitest rabbit anyone had ever seen. It was walking upright so everyone could see it had a soft, grey, furry tummy. Its kind face seemed full of laughter and it twitched its whiskers every now and again.

"Hello everybody!" called the Witch, "Please welcome my friend. Some call him the Easter Bunny, some the Great White Rabbit of Spring. But I know him as Cedric. I sometimes help him put out his chocolate eggs for you to find."

Cedric bowed to the assembled villagers.

"I have spoken to the bunnies," he said in a clear gentle voice. "And they say they are sorry they took those eggs. They said that they didn't realise they were for your party. But I think the pesky bunnies were too greedy to stop and think. They'll be here in a minute to give them all back."

"I hope they'll stay for the party," said Swampy to the white rabbit.

"I'm sure they will," smiled Cedric. "But they'll have to share the eggs with everyone else now. As they should have done before."

At that moment, a procession of fluffy rabbits bounced and hopped around the Boggles and each placed an egg into a huge basket which stood in the centre of the Easter Bunny's domed house.

Cedric gave each of them an approving pat on the head as they put the eggs back.

Then the party started. There were songs and dancing and there was food for everyone. The bunnies particularly liked the barkicrisps but they wouldn't touch any of the mudwort jelly. So Ticklechin ate it all. Then everyone lined up and one by one, they went into the Easter Bunny's house where they were each given a delicious chocolate egg. They were also allowed one wish to make, but it had to be a wish for someone else and not for themselves, or it wouldn't come true.

Minty and Mildred performed their synchronised swim, and this time the bubbles part went perfectly. Then the whole party formed a giant conga line and did a dance called the hippety-hop all evening.

As the sun finally set, Swampy lay down on a grassy bank and nibbled happily on the last of his delicious chocolate egg. He gazed at the final two or three dancers still twirling in the gloom. Behind them he could just make out a small group of bunnies sneaking off into the bushes dragging a huge sweetsludge pie behind them.

"Pesky bunnies" he muttered to himself, wondering if he should stop them.

But instead he smiled and raised his glass of butterfizz to the vanishing white bobbing tails. He hoped they liked the pie as much as he had liked the chocolate eggs.

Then he patted his round tummy and went off to find his bed.

The
End